THE DOMINIE WORLD OF
OCEAN LIFE

ANTARCTICA

MW00907759

Forests
in the Sea

WRITTEN & PHOTOGRAPHED
BY KIM WESTERSKOV, Ph.D.

🐚 Dominie Press, Inc.

1

Diving in a Kelp Forest

What's the best dive in the world? Diving on **tropical** coral reefs in warm, clear water? Diving with whales or dolphins? With sharks? In shipwrecks? In **Antarctica** under the sea ice? These are all wonderful dives, and I enjoyed each one of them, but perhaps my favorite dive would be somewhere different. For me, and many other divers around the world, there is nowhere more magical than a tall **kelp** forest in clear water.

There are about 100 different **species** of kelp living in cool seas around the world. Kelps are large brown seaweeds that often grow in dense underwater forests that are, in many ways, similar to forests on land. This hidden forest is just as full of life and wonder as a tropical rainforest on land. The feeling

◄ *Looking up toward the surface and sunlight through the tall, tall plants of a forest of giant kelp growing in water ninety-five feet deep. Many of the plants reach all the way from the rocky reefs on the bottom to the surface.*

In this photo you can see the three main parts of kelps: the holdfast, which attaches the kelp to the rock with some of the world's strongest glue; the stem; and the fronds, or leaves. ►

2

3

of wilderness and adventure is just as real, too. You can still find creatures not yet even described by science.

In a healthy forest of giant kelp, tall plants grow straight up from the rocky reef to the surface, often 100 feet above. Here the kelp spreads over the surface, forming a dense canopy.

One of the great things about these underwater forests is how easy they are to find. Kelp forests are found in shallow, cool seas around the world. They grow on rocky reefs in waters between forty-one and seventy-two degrees Fahrenheit. Kelp forests grow along the Pacific Coast of the United States, Canada, and Russia, the east coast of North America north of Cape Cod, southern Australia, South Africa, South America, New Zealand, the Atlantic coasts of northern Europe and Japan—and many other places with rocky coastlines and cool seas. Some of the world's finest kelp dives are off the coast of California. What about Alaska? Yes, rich kelp forests grow there, too, though we would need a good diving suit to keep warm!

2

The Sea's Fastest-Growing Plant

One of the most beautiful sights underwater is the golden growing tip of giant kelp dancing in an underwater current. Kelp blades are like the leaves of land plants. It is here that **photosynthesis** makes the food needed for the plants to grow. The sun supplies the energy, and seawater supplies the carbon dioxide and other **nutrients**. The food is then transported down through the stem to other parts of the plant.

Giant kelp is the fastest-growing plant in the sea, and maybe the fastest in the world. When conditions are right, kelp can grow at an amazing two feet per day or more. You can almost watch it grow!

This giant kelp washed up on the shore to surround two limpets on a rock. The beautiful growing tip is where the tiny new blades are produced. ▶

▲ *Kelp blades are like the leaves of land-based plants.*

◀ *A giant kelp forest reaches for the sun.*

Giant kelp can grow to 100 feet in just three months. On land, only a few of the 1,200 species of bamboo grow this quickly. Most kelp forests are in water from 15 to 100 feet deep.

Each kelp plant anchors itself to a rocky reef by a holdfast, a mass of finger-like haptera that fasten onto the rocks, using one of the strongest glues in the world.

From its holdfast, the giant kelp grows upward to the surface and then spreads out on the water, mixing with other kelp plants.

3

Underwater Forest Animals

Just as tropical rainforests on land support an amazing variety of life, so do the underwater kelp forests. Over 800 different species of animals live in the giant kelp forests off the California coast. The tangled holdfast of giant kelp is a favorite hideout for many animals. One scientist counted about

▲ *Some types of snails, such as this topshell, spend their lives crawling over kelp fronds as they drift with the currents and the waves. These snails are herbivores that feed on the kelp itself.*

23,000 small animals living in the holdfasts of five giant kelp plants. Most of the animals were snails, brittle stars, marine worms, crabs, and other crustaceans.

It usually looks peaceful down there in the kelp forest. But most

▲ *This is a healthy forest of Ecklonia kelp. Many of the animals living on the seafloor under the kelp forest are filter feeders that spend their lives firmly attached to the rocks. They get their food by straining the plankton from the seawater that always surrounds them. Common filter feeders include sponges, such as this massive black sponge, sea squirts and other ascidians, and moss animals, or bryozoans.*

◄ *An octopus prowls over the seafloor under a kelp forest. This predator is a master of camouflage, able to change its color in the blink of an eye. It not only changes to match the color of the reef or sand; it even copies the texture and shape of its surroundings.*

of the animals living in this crowded community are under the constant threat of being eaten. **Predators** are everywhere. Most predation happens slowly in underwater forests. A sea slug or snail may spend days eating a sponge or sea squirt.

The animals of the kelp forest can be divided into four groups, based on how they feed:

1. **Filter-feeders**: They get their food by straining the plankton from the seawater surrounding them.
2. **Herbivores**, or plant eaters: These animals feed on the kelp itself or on the drift seaweed that has broken off. They include snails, sea urchins, abalone, and a few fish.
3. **Carnivores**, or animal eaters: These include octopuses, most fish, many starfish, and some snails called whelks.
4. **Scavengers**: These animals roam over the **seafloor**, eating dead animals and plants as well as live **prey**.

A beautiful Diadema sea urchin nestles among patches of blue sea squirts. ▶

4

Fish in the Forest

Kelp forests are very important as fish nurseries, sheltering large numbers of juvenile fish of many species. A kelp forest creates **habitats** for many more kinds of fish than a rocky reef could support by itself. The kelp forest supplies both shelter and food.

Some fish spend their whole lives in kelp forests. Others are just visitors. John Dory, a species of fish, are found around the world in **temperate**

◀ *This scorpionfish is sitting in a bowl-like sponge in a clearing in the kelp forest. Although this one is easy to see, scorpionfish are often so well-camouflaged that divers do not see them. They can change color to blend in with the background. Scorpionfish are sometimes very aggressive toward divers, biting or butting them. Luckily their teeth are so small that they cannot do much damage.*

A colorful school of splendid perch swims over the kelp forest. ▶

seas, between warm **tropical** seas and cold polar seas. They are hunters, and are usually seen alone. They eat a variety of fish, which they **stalk**.

Some fish are so small or **camouflaged** so well that even experienced divers hardly ever see them. Others are big and obvious, such as the sharks or kingfish that sometimes prowl along the edges of the kelp forest.

Fish use camouflage both to hunt and to avoid being hunted. Smaller predators hide in the kelp and then ambush other fish. Some of these are shaped and colored to look like blades of kelp. To the hunted fish, these camouflaged predators are almost impossible to see.

Most of the fish in a kelp forest depend on the kelp in one way or another, but only a few species actually eat the kelp itself.

NOTES

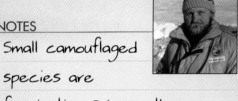

Small camouflaged species are fascinating. I know they are probably there, but often I cannot see them. On some dives I have spent hours just looking for these masters of camouflage. Once I was taking close-up photos of the seaweed itself before I saw a small fish about the size of my finger beautifully hidden in the seaweed and swaying with it.

▲ *This fur seal pup is playing with southern bull kelp on the shore.*

Mammals and Birds

In many kelp forests around the world, you are likely to meet sea lions or a local species of seal. Off the coast of California, you will meet the playful California sea lion and the harbor seal. In New Zealand, you will meet the New Zealand sea lion or the New Zealand fur seal. If we dived in the cool waters off South Australia or South Africa, we would meet still more species.

Seals and sea lions occasionally hunt in kelp forests, but mostly they use the kelp forests as a safe hideout from their enemies, the sharks. The most dangerous part of diving with sea lions or other seals is that they are a favorite food of great white sharks, which sometimes appear around seal or sea lion **colonies**.

Other marine **mammals** we meet in some kelp forests are whales and sea otters. Sea otters are found in small, widely spaced colonies living in giant kelp forests from Alaska down to California. Gray whales often swim through these same forests during their annual **migrations**. In the **southern hemisphere**, right whales come close to shore during their winter breeding season.

NOTES

Some of my best dives have been in kelp forests, swimming with sea lions or fur seals. Here, a sea lion swims straight toward me and then turns away. These sea lions played for hours in a giant kelp forest, sometimes with me, sometimes with one another. It was a gray, rainy day up above the water, but I made three scuba dives, each one right after the other, to enjoy and photograph these wonderful animals.

14

▲ *Rockhopper penguins come ashore at high speed to land on a rocky shoreline covered with southern bull kelp.*

An erect-crested penguin comes ashore on a steep, rocky shoreline past gold-colored southern bull kelp. ▶

Many kinds of birds are found around kelp forests, too. Birds feeding on the rich animal life of kelp forests include gulls, terns, herons, and cormorants or shags. Living in the kelp washed up on shorelines after storms are many types of small animals that feed a variety of shore birds and land birds. **Penguins** simply pass through kelp forests when they leave land for the sea and when they come ashore again.

6

Shallow Forests

Swimming off a rocky shore can be rewarding. Every square inch of rock usually has some animal or plant growing on it. Many sea animals and plants need to be attached to something solid. These species often grow on each other if there is no bare rock. Competition for space is intense here, and many of the animals have ways of discouraging other species from either settling on them or eating them. Chemical warfare is real down here, though usually it is fought in slow motion. Rocky reefs provide both shelter and food to many species of fish, too.

Exactly what you will see depends on where you live. In the tropics, you will find coral reefs but no swaying seaweeds. In cooler seas, you will most likely find the

◄ *Sea Urchins*

rocks covered by various types of seaweed. In deeper waters, some of the seaweed grows tall and forms forests. Close to shore in the shallows, they are not as tall, but they are still just as interesting.

▲ *This is an over-and-under view of a rocky shoreline. Underwater is a dense forest of shallow-water kelps.*

Many factors control exactly what you will find: sea temperature, nutrients in the water, shade and sunlight, weather, wave action, water clarity, the kinds of rocks, their shapes, and the inhabitants themselves. For example, sea urchins and other grazers may keep large areas free of large seaweeds.

There are three main kinds of seaweeds, based on the color of the **pigments** they use to photosynthesize. Green seaweeds have the same pigment, chlorophyll, that land plants use. Red and brown seaweeds have chlorophyll, too, but they also have other pigments that allow them to photosynthesize at lower light levels.

▲ *A fish swims past the ever-moving forest of shallow-water kelp.*

▲ *Kelp and a lawn of green seaweeds cover the rocks in shallow water.*

As a result, they can live deeper than the green seaweeds. The forest-forming seaweeds, or kelps, are all brown.

In kelp forests around the world, sea urchins are the major grazers on kelp. They normally eat the drift seaweed on the ocean floor or the small seaweeds growing there, but sometimes they become underwater lumberjacks, climbing up the kelp and chewing though the stem. The felled "tree" can then be eaten on the seafloor.

7

Bull Kelp
What's in a Name?

The bull kelp I know is a massive plant with a large, rubbery holdfast, a thick stem, and many long, flexible fronds that constantly **writhe** in the surf. The fronds are honeycombed with gas-filled spaces so the fronds float on the surface, where they absorb maximum sunlight for photosynthesis. Bull kelp also lives on surf-beaten rocky shores around southern Australia, Chile, and many sub-Antarctic islands.

If I lived on the Pacific Coast of North America, I would know "bull kelp," too. But this kelp

This forest of bull kelp was beautiful, but also dense and spooky. During this dive on a sub-Antarctic island, we were looking for an old shipwreck that has never been found. The survivors struggled ashore at night in 1864 somewhere near here. We never found any signs of the wreck. ▸

19

▲ *A New Zealand fur seal is seen in a dense bed of southern bull kelp.*

would look very different than the New Zealand one—because it would be a different species. From its holdfast, a long, thin stem rises up to a floating bulb from which grow many long blades. Unlike the shore-hugging bull kelp I know, this one lives out in deeper, calmer water. It is found from Alaska to California. Like giant kelp, it is one of the fastest-growing plants in the sea. The longest one measured was 118 feet in length, all from just one growing season.

That's the trouble with common names—and one of the reasons why we have scientific names. A common name in one place often means something quite different somewhere else. Some species have dozens of different common names, sometimes in different languages. And many plants and animals do not have any common names at all. Using scientific names gets around these problems. Whenever you use a scientific name, anyone else in the world, whatever language they speak, will know exactly which plant or animal you are talking about—as long as they know the scientific name.

The bull kelp in North America has only one scientific name, *Nereocystis luetkeana,* but many common names: ribbon kelp, giant kelp, bull whip kelp, bull kelp, bulb kelp, sea whip, sea kelp, horsetail kelp, bladder kelp, sea otter's cabbage, xopiikis, and kotka. The last two are

Some of the sub-Antarctic islands feature large, dense forests of bull kelp around their shorelines. Hundreds of rare, yellow-eyed penguins come ashore on this beach every night—and leave again the following morning. ▶

21

▲ *Southern bull kelp lives at or just below the low tide level on the most surf-lashed, wave-exposed coasts.*

Native American names. The bull kelp I know from New Zealand also has a number of common names, but its scientific name, *Durvillaea Antarctica,* tells us that it is a different species.

Scientific names are always in Latin and are written in *italics.* They have two parts and work pretty much like our own names. The first part of a scientific name is like a family name. So *Durvillaea* is like Westerskov. If we met *Durvillaea potatorum* in Australia, we would know that it was closely related to *Durvillaea Antarctica,* and the two would probably look alike.

8

People and Kelp

People have probably used seaweeds for as long as humans have lived by the sea. We know that the Chinese were using seaweeds as medicines as early as 3000 B.C. and have been eating them for at least 2,500 years.

Nearly all seaweeds are edible, though some taste better than others. They are rich in protein, minerals, and vitamins. People eat about 500 species of seaweed, and over 150 of those are commercially important. Seaweed is called *nori* in Japan. It is used in soups, to wrap sushi, and in many snacks. Nori has been grown in Tokyo Bay for 300 years.

Scuba divers are some of the biggest fans of kelp forests. Hundreds of thousands of divers explore these underwater forests each year. ▶

More than 500,000 tons of nori are grown on farms each year.

Millions of tons of seaweed are harvested from the sea each year: some farmed, some picked from the rocks, and some washed ashore after storms. The uses that we have found for seaweed are amazing.

If you live in North America, you probably use seaweed about fifteen times every day. It could be in the ice cream you eat, the clothes you wear, your toothpaste, even in the ink and paper in this book! You will find seaweed **extracts** in bread, cereals, chocolate milk, instant puddings, pickles, custard powder, pie fillings, salad dressing, soaps, beer, makeup, paint, detergents, shampoos, and medicines. It's a surprisingly long list!

Why are seaweed extracts so useful? Phycocolloids are the answer. *Phyco* means *seaweed,* and colloids are jelly-like or glue-like substances. They are large, complex molecules found in the cell walls of many types of seaweed. These seaweed extracts do many things: they make liquid foods thicker and smoother, they gel liquids, and they bind and stabilize liquids and prevent them from separating. They make breads soft and stop them from drying out. They make dried noodles stronger. Alginates make ice cream smooth and creamy, slow its melting, and prevent ice crystals from forming. And they are vital in medical and other scientific research. DNA fingerprinting involves the use of seaweed extracts.

Seaweeds are high in proteins and minerals; as a result, they are useful as food for humans and animals. In many coastal areas around the world, sheep and cattle eat seaweed on the beach. Some of them live almost entirely on seaweed. And farmers and gardeners the world over know that seaweed is an excellent fertilizer.

Beyond the Kelp

Deep on the rocky reef, where there is not enough light for kelp and other seaweeds to grow, we find gardens of plant-like animals. They look nothing like the animals we see on land—they don't move, but they are hungry. Sponges of many kinds dominate the deep reef. Massive sponges spread far over the rock, and large branching sponges reach up into the current.

Sponges often form shrubs or low gardens. Most species are small, but some can grow to six feet in height. They feed by drawing a current of water in through small holes in their surface, filtering out the plankton, and then passing the water out through larger holes.

◀ *This deep reef is colorful and bursting with life of many kinds. Fish swim above the garden of yellow finger sponges, pink gorgonian fans, yellow and orange golf-ball sponges, and many other deep reef creatures. These deep reef gardens form an important habitat for fish and other reef inhabitants.*

▲ *Living black corals, which are really colonies of thousands of individual polyps, are white.*

▲ *Black coral colonies create habitats for other animals, such as these snakestars, here seen with their thin arms wrapped tightly around the coral branches.*

Some sponges can filter 1,000 times their own weight in water every hour. A few other animals eat sponges, but most predators avoid them because they have splinters of glass or rubbery fibers throughout their bodies and they produce **toxic** chemicals.

Gorgonian fans, black corals, hydroid trees—all colonies of coral-like animals—also grow in colorful undersea gardens. The deep reef is one of my favorite diving places. For me, the color and drama down there are as magnificent as a coral reef.

◄ *A garden of yellow finger sponges grows on a deep reef. Much like plants on land, or the kelp forests we've already seen, these animal gardens form a habitat—a place where other species can live.*

Think of seawater as drifting soup, and you will realize why so many sea animals have taken to a life of sitting glued to a rock, or anything hard, including other animals, seaweeds, shipwrecks, etc. Then they simply wait and let their meals come to them. All they have to do is catch their food as it drifts by.

Imagine for a minute that you are one of these sea animals living on a rocky reef. To be successful with living there, the main thing is to grab some space on the rock and glue yourself to it. Then, if possible, you need to reach up to where there is more food in the faster water flow. There will be other animals trying to push you out, grow on top of you, or eat you, so you will need a good defense strategy, too.

Much of the killing and competition on the reef is in slow motion, but it's vicious all the same. To stay alive, you will need sturdy armor —thick, leathery skin or a hard skeleton—and stinging cells, used to catch plankton, defend yourself, and make you taste terrible. Some nasty poisons for chemical warfare would be very useful, too.

10

Coral Reef Gardens

In warm tropical seas, we find spectacular underwater gardens. There are seaweeds here, but they are the smaller red and green seaweeds, not the large brown kelps—it is too warm for them here. Our first dives on a coral reef are exciting, but confusing. There is just so much happening—so much color and activity.

Like kelp forests, coral reefs provide many habitats for other organisms—it's just that most of the corals are hard and rigid, unlike the flexible, ever-moving kelps. In many ways, a coral reef is like an underwater city. The "apartments" and other "buildings" are the corals. Each coral mound, or coral tree, is a colony of thousands of small

Shaped like an oversized ball, this large cabbage coral is home for hundreds of small, colorful fish. As I approached, they hid among the folds of the coral. ▶

▲ *Unlike hard corals and sea fans, soft corals such as this have no hard skeleton.*

▲ *This is a spectacular underwater garden of sea fans, each up to six feet across. The largest sea fans found by divers are about twice this size, and, very rarely, three times as large.*

animals called polyps. Each polyp makes a small, hard cup of calcium carbonate, which it hides in when it is inactive or threatened. These cups are cemented together, making up a coral colony that looks more like stone than a colony of animals. So what we call "a coral" is all the old cups cemented together, plus a layer of polyps in their cups spread over the outside.

Polyps look like small sea anemones, with a ring of **tentacles** around a central mouth. The tentacles are used for defense and to capture small animals for food. Coral polyps are so small that you could easily miss them. Many stony coral polyps are the size of a pinhead or the head of a small nail—less than $1/10$ of an inch. The largest are a little over an inch in diameter.

Tropical seas are great to dive in because they are warm, and the water is so clear. But the water is clear because there is very little food in it. The coral reef is like an oasis in an underwater desert. And what feeds the amazing variety and richness of life we see on the coral reef? The answer is surprising.

Coral polyps can feed in two very different ways. Many feed at night, catching small plankton as it drifts by. But most reef-building corals also have tiny algae living inside them.

Just like seaweeds, these tiny algae use sunlight to make food and provide the polyp with oxygen. In many reef-building corals, these algae produce enough food for themselves, and for much of the coral's needs. The coral polyps, in return, provide the algae with carbon dioxide and other wastes, which are nutrients to the algae, and a safe home. Such a relationship, where both parties benefit, is called **symbiotic**.

Coral reefs are found in warm, clear, shallow waters of tropical oceans around the world. Since the corals depend on the algae growing inside them, and these algae need sunlight, the corals rarely grow in water deeper than about 150 feet.

Glossary

Antarctica:	An uninhabited continent surrounding the South Pole
Camouflage:	A device used by some animals to blend into their surroundings in order to avoid being seen by predators or prey
Carnivores:	Animals that eat other animals
Colonies:	Groups of animals of the same kind that live together and are dependent on one another
Extracts (n):	Materials or solutions removed from a plant and used in a variety of products
Habitats:	Places where animals and plants live and grow
Herbivores:	Animals that eat plants
Kelp:	Seaweed that grows where currents of water constantly wash its fronds, or giant leaves; plants that form vast underwater groves and kelp forests
Mammals:	A class of warm-blooded animals in which the female feeds the young with its own milk
Migrations:	The movement of large numbers of animals from one region or habitat to another in response to cyclical seasonal changes
Nutrients:	Materials that provide nourishment and help animals and humans to stay healthy and grow
Penguins:	Flightless, web-footed seabirds that use their flipper-shaped wings for swimming
Photosynthesis:	A process by which plants or plantlike organisms use sunlight to make food/energy
Pigments:	Natural coloring that occurs in some animals and plants
Predators:	Animals that hunt, catch, and eat other animals
Prey (n):	Animals that are hunted and eaten by other animals
Scavengers:	Animals that eat dead plants and animals, along with live prey
Seafloor:	The surface of the Earth at the bottom of the sea
Southern Hemisphere:	The half of the Earth located south of the equator
Species:	Types of animals that have some physical characteristics in common
Stalk (v):	To quietly and secretly follow someone or something
Symbiotic:	Characteristic of a mutually beneficial relationship
Temperate:	Mild; marked by a moderate climate
Tentacles:	Long, flexible organs used to catch and hold prey
Toxic:	Poisonous
Tropical:	Characteristic of areas of land and sea that are very warm and humid throughout the year
Writhe:	To move with graceful twists and turns